ST. TIGGYW...
WILDLIFE HOSPITAL

Lucky the Little Owl
and other stories

First published in Great Britain by
Collins in 1996

1 3 5 7 9 8 6 4 2

Collins is a division of
HarperCollins*Publishers* Ltd,
77-85 Fulham Palace Road,
Hammersmith, London W6 8JB

Printed and bound in Great Britain
by Caledonian International Book Manufacturing Ltd.,
Glasgow, G 64

ISBN 0 00 675210 1

ST. TIGGYWINKLES
WILDLIFE HOSPITAL

Lucky the Little Owl
and other stories

Les Stocker

Collins
An Imprint of HarperCollins*Publishers*

Also by Les Stocker

Jaws the Hedgehog and other stories

Contents

Introduction

These stories tell of some of the animal characters who became firm favourites with the nurses and volunteers at St. Tiggywinkles Wildlife Hospital. Sue, Colin and I, together with our great friends the staff at St. Tiggywinkles, take in and care for thousands of sick or injured wild animals every year.

These animals can be mammals, birds, amphibians, reptiles... even fish, but they are all just as important to us. The animals get better through their own courage and with a little help from us. Whenever possible that great moment comes when they are released back into the wild. Meet the animals, through these stories, and understand why I am so privileged to have known them.

People at St. Tiggywinkles

Les, Sue and Colin Stocker	Founders and Directors
Dr John Lewis	Specialist veterinary consultant
Peter Kertesz	Animal dentist
Lisa Frost	Animal Services Officer
Lia Titman	Junior veterinary nurse
Jane Ravie	Junior veterinary nurse

Plus dozens of volunteers

Bob the Fox

Foxes are amazing animals. One that I met, called Bob, showed me just how clever they are. Bob lived on an Air Force base where not only did he benefit from the full protection of armed guards, but he also fed like a king on buns and tit-bits given to him by the airmen. He had to look nowhere else for a livelihood and could have lived there quite comfortably for the rest of his life. But, like all foxes, Bob was inquisitive. He strayed outside the protection of his own personal army and promptly got into trouble.

Perhaps he had got a little too fat and slow in his nice easy lifestyle, for as soon as he had climbed over the base fence, two big dogs set upon him and gave him a sound beating. Somehow he had managed to escape and clamber back to the safety of his home, but he was severely injured. Dave Frost, an airman and the husband of Lisa, our Animal Services Officer, found Bob and called me to help him, if I could.

When I arrived, Bob could hardly walk and was crawling around on his knees. He was bleeding from wounds all over his body and his once proud tail was torn to shreds. I could tell that he was close to dying for, as I crept up to him, he made no attempt to escape. Gently I picked him up by the scruff of his neck, just in case he made a last-

ditch attempt to bite me. He didn't. He
lay there limp and lifeless as I put him into a
carrying case.

Bob was looking very sorry for himself as
I carried him to the car. His friends were
worried about him and came to see him off.

"We'd love to have him back when he's
better," said Dave. I nodded, but really I
had my doubts about keeping him alive.

All the way back to St. Tiggywinkles Bob
just lay as though he was dead, but every
now and again a big, sad sigh let me know
that he was hanging on.

At last, back at the hospital, I took him
into the prep room, where all new casualties
are taken to receive any live-saving
treatments we can give them. While the
nurses and I got all the medicines together,
Dr John Lewis, our consultant vet,
examined Bob's injuries. He was as cold as

ice. We set up an intravenous drip to get him over the shock of his capture and to warm him up. It would also replace a lot of the blood Bob had lost from his wounds.

John cleaned Bob's wounds and said that they should heal very quickly provided he received a course of antibiotics to keep down any infection. He was really worried about the wrist joint on Bob's front leg and put on a plaster cast to give it strength. The plaster cast is a special bandage that is softened with water and wound around an injured leg. It sets hard within minutes and stops any injuries from moving so that they do not hurt as much and can start to heal. I then covered the plaster in a bright red bandage, to keep it clean, while John had a good look at Bob's tail. It had been bitten right through. It would never heal, so using a local anaesthetic injection, like dentists use, John snipped through the one piece of skin that was holding it on. This left Bob with a short stumpy tail just like a boxer dog's. I wondered how poor Bob was going to feel about losing his tail. Some foxes can get very upset.

Bob was now starting to get warmer. He was obviously quite used to people, because when he realised where he was, he did not panic like foxes do normally. Instead, he just lay quietly in the warmth looking at all of us as if to say, "Thank you for taking care of me."

When he was all bandaged and stitched up we took him through to our large mammal ward where he could rest and recover in a nice secure cage. The intravenous drip we had fitted fed life-saving fluids into him but in true fox fashion he took one look at the clear plastic tubing

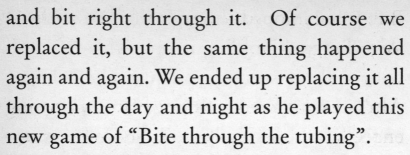

and bit right through it. Of course we replaced it, but the same thing happened again and again. We ended up replacing it all through the day and night as he played this new game of "Bite through the tubing".

By the following morning, Bob was much better. He was sitting up and talking to me in little grunts and whines, and I could have sworn he was grinning at me.

His short stumpy tail did not seem to bother him. The only thing that did upset him was the visit from the dentist. All our animals have their teeth checked. Just like us, if there is any damage or tooth decay then a toothache may stop them being able to eat. Peter Kertesz is a dentist for humans but also looks after animals. And while Dr John gave Bob an anaesthetic, so that he would sleep, Peter sorted out Bob's broken teeth and also gave him some root fillings.

Bob would not have any tooth trouble for a long, long while.

After several weeks, Bob was fit and strong enough to go home. Early one warm evening, I took him out with Lisa and her husband Dave. Dave knew Bob's favourite spot amongst the trees and undergrowth on the hill above the airbase. We opened up the carrying box and let him go.

At first, Bob sniffed around the box and along the path edges. He went off and came back and walked round and round us, gradually getting further away. Then he seemed to pick up an interesting scent and ghosted into the darkness and was gone. We felt relieved that Bob was back home and would never need rescuing again. How wrong can you be?

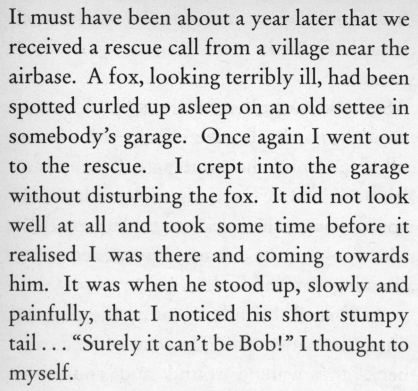

It must have been about a year later that we received a rescue call from a village near the airbase. A fox, looking terribly ill, had been spotted curled up asleep on an old settee in somebody's garage. Once again I went out to the rescue. I crept into the garage without disturbing the fox. It did not look well at all and took some time before it realised I was there and coming towards him. It was when he stood up, slowly and painfully, that I noticed his short stumpy tail . . . "Surely it can't be Bob!" I thought to myself.

Then, as he almost fell off the settee, I knew it was him. He had a slight limp at the wrist where those dogs had injured him last year. But the rest of him did not look a bit like Bob. All his fine red coat had gone and his back and haunches were covered with sore-looking scabs. His eyes, which were once so bright, now looked like small painful slits as he tried to make out who I was.

Somehow after we released him twelve months ago, Bob had picked up a disease called sarcoptic mange. Mange is caused by a tiny spider-like creature called a mite. Bob would have had millions eating into his skin. He would not recover until we killed all of them off with an injection.

As I gently picked Bob up and carried him to the car, I wondered if he knew it was me. All the way back to St. Tiggys I could hear his little grunts and whines as he told me his troubles.

Everybody was pleased to see Bob again, and also upset at how he looked. But all of them had seen mange cases before, and knew that, after his treatment, in a few days the scabs would fall off and Bob would start growing new fur. Once again I put Bob on an intravenous drip, and also gave him an injection that would kill all those mites.

For the first few days he looked very, very sad as he lay huddled in a warm cage in our large mammal ward. He would still whimper his little grunts and whines but seemed too sore to stand up and eat. But gradually over the next week the injection took effect and all the mites died. Bob started to look and feel better and was not scratching himself any more, but was scratching at the cage, to get out.

The weather was not too bad so finally I gave in and put him outside into one of the badger pens which had a little hut at one end to sleep in, and a wired-off area where he could feed and exercise.

This time he was really spoilt by everybody. He was fed with grapes, and given the best doggy foods anyone could buy, and on Saturdays, Ann, one of our volunteers, would share her Marmite sandwiches with him. It would take him about two months to get all his fur back and as it was getting towards winter I did not want him to go until he had a nice full warm coat.

Unfortunately, Bob had other ideas. One morning I looked out and saw that his pen door was open. I rushed down there, hoping he was still inside, but he'd gone. He was such a clever animal, he must have decided he wanted to be free again and somehow slid open the catch on the door.

Immediately I got everybody searching the hospital grounds, diving under every hedgerow and clump of vegetation. There was no sign of him. I was worried. Bob had escaped into an unfamiliar countryside over

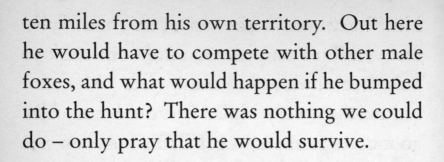

ten miles from his own territory. Out here he would have to compete with other male foxes, and what would happen if he bumped into the hunt? There was nothing we could do – only pray that he would survive.

We thought we had seen the last of Bob. But a few days later, Chris Patterson, who works with Sue in our office, phoned to say that there was a fox with no tail raiding her bird table. Chris lived just a short way from the air base. It couldn't possibly be Bob again – or could it?

Sue and I jumped in the car and sped over to Chris's. By the time we got there the fox had gone, but Chris was certain it was Bob.

"I remember him well. I used to give him Smarties," she told me. "He still hasn't got all his fur."

I decided that I must catch Bob and take

him back to make sure he was fully recovered from the mange and fit enough to face the winter ahead.

Foxes are very clever and do not usually go into cage traps, but I had a trick up my sleeve. The following night, I put some Marmite sandwiches in the trap. Chris said it was about eleven o'clock when she heard the clunk as the door to the trap shut. When she went out to look, there was Bob munching away at his Marmite sandwiches and looking as if he had won a Marmite lottery.

Back at St. Tiggywinkles again, he was again treated like an honoured guest. He got extra Marmite, and I know that Chris slipped him the occasional handful of Smarties on the quiet. After a couple of weeks, all his fur had grown back, and he was looking fit and ready to go. I put him in a new, much larger area where he could exercise. But can you believe it, once more the sly old thing found his way out and completely disappeared. Was this the last time we would ever see Bob? Was it heck!

Three days later Sue received a call from a lady who lived near the air base, "There's a fox lying on top of my hedge. He's making all sorts of funny groany, whiny sounds, as if to say 'Let's be friends'."

Sue called me from the bottom of the field where I was planning new fencing to stop any more animals getting out. "Not Bob again!" I groaned when I heard the news. But I knew by now that Bob was capable of anything. He was obviously enjoying his game of hide and seek!

I raced through the windy, twisting roads to see this fox for myself. Sure enough, there was Bob as large as life and fit as a fiddle, lying on top of a hedge and grinning from ear to ear. He gave me a look as if to say, "Oh no, not him again," then in a flash he was off the hedge and down a path between the houses. He disappeared through a gap between two garages. He obviously knew his way around. I searched for him for nearly an hour but I never found him.

Chris still sees Bob raiding her bird table. He now has a foxy girlfriend. I still expect every call for a fox rescue in that area to be Bob, but thankfully, he seems to be keeping out of trouble. I've no doubt I'll be seeing the old rascal before too long, though, and I hope when I do, it'll be Marmite sandwiches and Smarties he's after, and not because he's in trouble again.

Lucky the Little Owl

Lucky was brought in one summer's evening by Peter Johnson. Peter and his father were walking their dog in a local wood when they found the little owl trapped by his leg in an old log. They had carefully pulled his leg free, and brought Lucky to St. Tiggywinkles wrapped up in a jumper. Lucky lay quietly in the jumper just glaring at Peter, who held him on his lap. He did not even attack Peter with his talons as owls often do. He was very weak.

Jane, one of our nurses, called me and I had my first look at Lucky. He was a young little owl; I could tell by the fluffy grey down still on his head. In the wild in Britain there are five types of owl. None of them are very big but for some reason the smallest of them all is known simply as "the little owl". It is not much bigger than a blackbird.

Lucky glared at me with his golden yellow unblinking stare, as if to say, "I'm not frightened of you. I could get away if I wanted to."

As I lifted him I noticed immediately that he could not see out of his left eye. But even worse, both his wings were hanging useless at his sides and one leg was pointing hideously back to front. Owls have very sharp talons that they use to catch their prey, and defend themselves. It's safer to wear gloves when handling them but I find I can treat them much better without them. Mind you, I am very, very careful.

Like many naughty baby owls, Lucky had probably climbed out of the hole in the tree where his nest was. Most babies manage to climb back in but Lucky must have fallen, bashing his young wings on branches on the way down and breaking them. He had then got his foot jammed in a log and broken his leg trying to get himself free. As he was too young to fly he was very lucky not to have been killed in the fall. And even more lucky that no other animals had come along and eaten him. Now you know how he got his name!

Jane gave him some medicines to make him feel better. First there was a very big pill that he would have to have twice every day. This would clear up any infection in

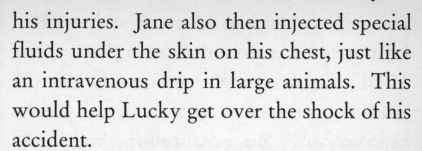

his injuries. Jane also then injected special fluids under the skin on his chest, just like an intravenous drip in large animals. This would help Lucky get over the shock of his accident.

Now I needed to X-ray him to find out exactly which bones he had broken and work out a way of treating them. He was not happy as I picked him up. He fixed his staring yellow eyes on me and clacked his beak, rather like the "clip clop" of a horse's hooves. As he grabbed one of my fingers fiercely with the talons on his uninjured leg I knew, and felt, that it was this brave spirit that had kept him alive in that wood. I laid him carefully on the X-ray plate and he gripped my finger even tighter, forcing his razor-sharp talons into my skin. He was surprisingly strong for such a little bird, and I hadn't been careful enough.

X-raying wild animals is very tricky, because just like in human hospitals we have to be outside the X-ray room when the button is pressed, and the animal has to keep very still. But you cannot say to a wild bird, "Hold it", or "Take a deep breath", or even, "Watch the birdie." As soon as you let go of them they move or struggle and ruin the picture. Lucky was just the same. Each time I went out of the room he would jump up and stare after me defiantly as if to say, "Don't think you're going to get a photograph of me!"

There was nothing for it. I had to hold him in place under the camera with bits of sticky tape. He looked at me in disgust. But – third time lucky – I managed to press the button while he was still. Then I congratulated him on being such a good model, and put him in a warm box while

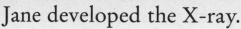

Jane developed the X-ray.

It turned out to be a good X-ray and we could see clearly that Lucky had broken two bones in his left wing and three bones in his right wing as well as the bone in his right leg. I was now really worried whether he would ever be able to fly. But a bird's bones will heal very quickly and with Lucky's spirit and some good splints to stop the broken bones moving, he had a good chance.

Very gently and carefully I dealt with each fracture in turn. Feeling along his wings I found the broken bones and lined them up so that they would heal as straight as possible. Each one was then wrapped in splints made from a Weetabix box and held in place with coloured bandages.

The broken leg needed extra care, as owls use their feet to catch their prey. In the wild, little owls catch beetles and other small animals and will even eat worms. If the leg did not heal properly, Lucky would never be able to hunt again. To splint a bird's leg I use a lolly stick wrapped with extra-sticky plaster tape. In humans a broken leg is put into a plaster cast but one of these would have been too heavy for Lucky to lift.

Now, with all his colourful bandages on, Lucky looked like a Christmas tree. He had been very brave, but was not at all amused and looked at me as if he would like to wrap *me* up in bandages from head to foot!

His damaged eye would have to be looked at by our consultant vet, Dr John Lewis. This was not so much of a worry because owls can still hunt even though they may be blind in one eye. Owls do a lot of their hunting by sound and have ears specially adapted for this purpose. Even when they are feeding, they close their eyes and feel their food with the whiskers around their beaks.

Now, after his ordeal, it was time for Lucky to be tucked up in a nice warm cage in our bird intensive care ward. We offered him some food but he was not interested. He just blinked at us and turned his head away.

For three days he flatly refused to eat, even though we offered him the best owl food you can get: chopped mice that we buy frozen from an animal food supermarket. He just crouched grumpily in the corner of his cage. I was worried. He was only a little bird and could not go without food for much longer.

By the fourth day, I knew I was going to have to force him to eat. I got some gooey pieces of chopped mice all ready, then I held him firmly in my left hand, pushed open his beak and popped a piece in. He grabbed my finger with his good foot and promptly spat the piece of mouse out. I tried again, this time pushing that tasty morsel a little further into his mouth. Still he spat it out. The next time, I pushed the meat right back into his throat with a cotton bud. Success – he closed his eyes and in three tremendous gulps, swallowed it right down and was glaring at me, daring me to try it again!

It took ages to get just six pieces of mouse into him. He looked miserable, and flatly refused to take any more, but at last he had some food inside him to give him the strength to get better.

Now we had to wait. All birds of prey, including owls, eat whole animals and insects. They cannot digest the fur and bone of animals or the hard outer skeleton of insects. Some time after they have eaten, all this indigestible material is formed into a pellet in their stomachs and then coughed up. If they do not bring up a pellet then something is wrong with their digestive system.

We waited anxiously all that evening. Then just after supper Jane came running in, "He's done it! He's brought up a pellet. He's going to be all right!"

Ever cautious I said, "Let's wait and see. This is only the first meal. There are still all sorts of things that can go wrong."

For the next four days we left food in his cage, but he never touched it. We had to go through the ritual of hand-feeding him and waiting for the pellet. Then one morning we found his pieces of mice gone, and there, lying in his cage, was a bright new pellet.

From now on he would feed himself. We were over the first major hurdle to his recovery!

Each week I changed his splints and exercised his wing and leg joints to stop them getting stiff. His wings mended beautifully. After three weeks I left them uncovered so he could exercise them for himself.

After five weeks his broken leg had healed too. It was slightly crooked but at least he could now use his toes on that foot. At first he tried his talons out on my fingers again but luckily for me he would still need to exercise them before they were as crushing as his other foot!

John, the vet, confirmed that sadly he would never be able to see out of his damaged eye, but we could now go ahead with putting Lucky in an outside aviary so that he could learn to fly.

In the wild, Lucky would have been able to fly by now. After he had climbed out of the nest on the day of his accident, he should have joined his brothers and sisters in practising jumping from one branch to the other. This way, he would have learnt to fly a little bit at a time.

But Lucky had not been so lucky, and had missed the branch on his first try. He now had a lot more feathers so should find it easier to take off. Mind you, all his joints were stiff where he had not used them for so long. Sue and I watched his efforts through a peep-hole in the door of his aviary.

On his first attempt he climbed up on to a perch and took off. His mended wings were still very stiff and he plummeted down on to the thick grass underneath him. He had plenty of feathers so the fall would not

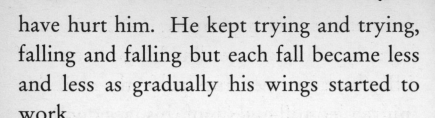

have hurt him. He kept trying and trying, falling and falling but each fall became less and less as gradually his wings started to work.

His first actual flight saw him take off and fly straight into the wire mesh of his aviary. It was so good to see him actually fly. Some people say that a bird with a broken wing will never fly again. Lucky had proved them all wrong. He got a bloody nose but he was happy! He had proved that he could fly and from now on he would only get stronger.

His success in the air obviously went to his head. He started to boss around the other little owls in his aviary by glaring at them, and even managed to climb to the highest perch which made him "king pin", the dominant bird.

I will not release him for some time yet,

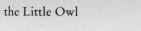

not until he can fly perfectly and his injured leg can grab my finger like his good one. If I find that he never flies perfectly, or if that injured leg still gives him trouble, I will not release him into the wild. Instead, I will make sure that he has a full natural life in one of our large aviaries with a steady flow of other injured little owls for him to boss around!

The Glis glis and the Postbox

It had not been a good day for George the postman. He had had a puncture in the middle of the rush-hour traffic in Wendover, and now his red Post Office van coughed and spluttered as it struggled up the hill out of the village. This was to be his third call of the day to empty a small postbox set in a wall along the hillside road known as the "Switchback". His little van definitely did not fancy the ups and downs of this road and threatened to stop each time it reached the top of a slope.

Finally with a last, "chug, chug", his van gave up and started to roll backwards, much to the horror of the queue of traffic behind. Only at the last minute did George manage to swing his steering wheel and come to a halt on the grass verge.

He would now have to walk back to Wendover to phone his manager and tell him he had broken down. But first, he would empty the Switchback postbox.

Getting his mailbag and key from the van, George climbed up the hill to the postbox. He put his key in the lock and heard a familiar "clunk" as he turned it. But as he opened the door, a horrific noise from inside made him slam it shut and jump back. "Whirr! Whirr! Whirr!" It sounded like a motorbike that would not start. What on earth was it? It must be some kind of animal – a strange snake, maybe, or a nest of angry wasps or bees?

As quietly as possible, George slid open the lock and peered through the gap in the half-open door into the gloom inside. "Whirr! Whirr! Whirr!" He jumped back as the noise got louder. He was frightened now, but determined to find out what it was, so he opened the door a little more. He could just make out the pile of letters all ripped to shreds. "Whirr! Whirr! Whirr!" Out of the dark came the noise again. George caught sight of some big white teeth and bright glowing eyes. He slammed the door shut and locked it quickly, once and for all. He didn't know what it was, but he wasn't going to risk finding out. Nor was he going to risk taking the mail – it would just have to stay there!

He threw his mailbag into his van and walked back to Wendover to phone his manager, muttering along the way. "It must be a squirrel, but then squirrels bite. Let the manager get bitten!"

His manager knew how squirrels can bite and decided that rather than risk his own fingers, it was time to call St. Tiggywinkles to the rescue.

We are quite used to wild animals and all of them would take great delight in biting us if they could. For small animals like squirrels we use extra thick welders' gloves to protect ourselves. But I had my doubts that this was a squirrel. Knowing the area I thought it was more likely to be a Glis glis which I also knew had a fearsome bite. They are grey and are not unlike small squirrels, but they are much prettier with big ears, long white whiskers and big, black eyes that let them see at night when they normally come out to feed. They live in trees like squirrels but when they want to nest they choose buildings or other man-made nestboxes like fuse boxes, bird boxes, garden sheds and, evidently, postboxes! They are of the dormouse family and just like their small cousin the dormouse in Alice in Wonderland, they spend a lot of their lives curled up in their furry tails, fast asleep.

Lisa and I met George and the Post Office manager by the postbox. George told me his tale, and I put on my thick gloves ready for anything. It all seemed nice and quiet until the manager put his key in the door and clunked it open.

"Whirr! Whirr! Whirr!" came from inside. I had heard the sound many times before and said to Lisa, "Not a very happy

Glis glis."

The manager jumped out of the way as I slowly opened the door. The whirring noise got louder and then I could see this brave little Glis glis standing up on its haunches, with its big ears flattened back as it shouted at me. Its front legs were made into fists as though it was going to punch me but I did not give it a chance, and in a flash grabbed it around the body.

It bit me. Glis glis always do and even through thick gloves I could feel its sharp teeth break into my finger. But in spite of the pain I did not let go of the angry little animal – and it did not let go of me! As quickly as I possibly could I slipped my hand into the plastic carrying box Lisa had ready, shook the Glis glis off my finger with difficulty, and slammed the lid shut.

Then I went back to the postbox to pull

out all the mail our Glis glis had torn up to make its nest. There were letters, bills and even a cheque ripped to pieces by its sharp teeth. But there was something else, too. As I lifted the first clump out I uncovered a pile of pink wriggling animals. Our Glis glis was a mum and had made a nursery for her babies amongst all the post!

We had to get them out without leaving any human scent, as this might upset their mother, so even though they have no teeth, Lisa put on some gloves. She carefully picked out the babies, who looked just like tiny pink sausages, and put them into the plastic carrying case with their mother. Altogether there were eight.

Our main worry was that after all the disturbance Mrs Glis might not take them back. If she didn't, we would have to hand-rear them all on miniature babies' bottles.

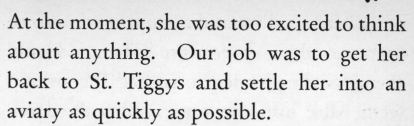

At the moment, she was too excited to think about anything. Our job was to get her back to St. Tiggys and settle her into an aviary as quickly as possible.

We drove off leaving George the postman and his manager trying to sort out the broken-down van and a jigsaw of tattered post.

Back at St. Tiggywinkles we set up a small mobile aviary for Mrs Glis and her family. We put in branches, a new nest box and piles of dried leaves that she could use as nest material. I also put in a bowl of chopped apples, which are Glis glis's all-time favourite food.

When everybody else had gone out of the room, I gently slid the carrying case into the aviary. I took off the lid and laid it on its side so that Mrs Glis could easily get out. She did not need any encouragement. She

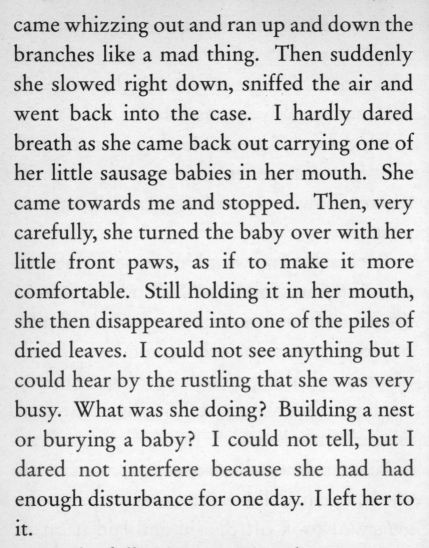

came whizzing out and ran up and down the branches like a mad thing. Then suddenly she slowed right down, sniffed the air and went back into the case. I hardly dared breath as she came back out carrying one of her little sausage babies in her mouth. She came towards me and stopped. Then, very carefully, she turned the baby over with her little front paws, as if to make it more comfortable. Still holding it in her mouth, she then disappeared into one of the piles of dried leaves. I could not see anything but I could hear by the rustling that she was very busy. What was she doing? Building a nest or burying a baby? I could not tell, but I dared not interfere because she had had enough disturbance for one day. I left her to it.

By the following morning there were no babies left in the carrying case. As I

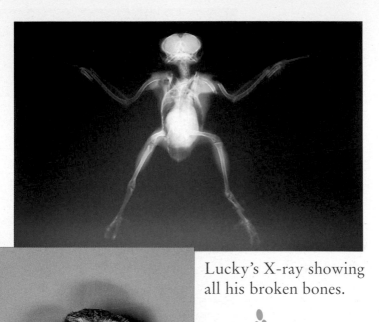

Lucky's X-ray showing all his broken bones.

The little owl with his wings in plaster...

... and getting stronger in an outside aviary.

Deidre looks sweet
and gentle... but
fights like a tiger.

Deidre stands
guard...

... until she's sure
it's safe to attend to
her baby.

Bob is clever and handsome and he *loves* Marmite sandwiches!

Bob is strong enough to go home – even with his short stumpy tail.

One last look at his carrying box... then Bob slowly ambles off.

Rudolf has knobbly brown skin...

... and a red, lumpy nose.

Lisa takes the baby Glis glis from the postbox.

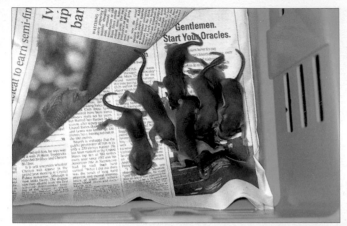

What news! Eight little wriggling babies to feed.

Mother Glis glis in her temporary nest.

As the Glis glis babies grow up, their nest box gets a bit crowded.

It's time to venture out into the strange world outside the nest box.

Bernard, Ed and Matt – three great friends who met at St. Tiggywinkles.

Les and Sue, enjoying a well deserved break!

carefully moved the piles of dry leaves apart there were no babies there either. There was only one place they could be – in the new nest box. It was dark in there, so with a tiny torch I quickly had a peek. There she was: clever Mrs Glis lying down with all her eight babies happily suckling her milk. It could not have been better. Hopefully all we had to do now was give her peace and quiet and plenty of food. She would do the rest.

Eight babies were a lot to rear so we all made sure that over the next few weeks Mrs Glis had plenty of her favourite apples and other food to give her the energy to make her babies big and strong. We saw no sign of the babies until, late one Sunday night some weeks later, Lia burst into the staff room.

"I've seen them! I've seen the babies!"

she blurted out. Before she could say any more we had all pushed past her, and run quietly down the corridor to the aviary. There, poking out of a hole in the side of the nest box, was a tiny pointed face with big black eyes and long white whiskers. Another baby was looking out of the main entrance hole. And then a third, climbing over his brother's back to peer at the strange world outside his nest box. Mrs Glis was trying to keep them under control, and pull them back into the nest box, but baby number three managed to get right out of the nest box and on to one of the branches. He stopped and swayed as if he was surprised to have so much space around him. I thought he was going to fall, but somehow he managed to hang on and climb back into the safety of the box.

That was obviously enough adventure for

one night because they didn't come out again. But the following night, when I crept in, there were baby Glis glis all over the aviary. They were climbing, exploring and fighting over bits of pear, which they seemed to like even better than apple. I tried to count them. It was pretty difficult, but I eventually made it to eight. Mrs Glis had done a brilliant job in bringing up such healthy youngsters. She must have been worn out. No wonder she stayed in the nest box and slept while they were all out playing.

Now they are a lot bigger and live with their mother in a big indoor aviary. It's getting towards winter and as dormice, like hedgehogs, hibernate through the colder months we like to keep them in to protect them from the ice and snow.

By next spring they will all be the same

size and we will not be able to tell Mrs Glis from her babies, or for that matter any of the other Glis glis that will share their aviary.

I could not help thinking that George's postbox was an ideal nest box for another Glis glis family. I only hope that next year perhaps the Post Office will try to make it Glis-proof so that we do not have to disturb another mother with her babies.

Rudolf, the Red-Nosed Toad

The cold winter weather usually sends a lot of casualties to St. Tiggywinkles. Freezing conditions catch out all sorts of creatures: hedgehogs who are too small to survive; herons and kingfishers who find their favourite feeding ponds frozen over, and even tiny little bats who have flown from their nice, warm homes only to get blown off course by an icy blast of wind. But we never expect to see any frogs and toads, who should all be sound asleep in the mud at the bottom of frozen pools or safely tucked up under a nice, cosy rock.

Rudolf, for some reason known only to himself, had to be different. He had decided to go for a walk (toads walk, they do not hop like frogs) on Christmas Eve. That is when his troubles started, and how he got his name.

Penny, one of the volunteers who help us at St. Tiggys, was out walking her two great, shaggy Old English sheepdogs, Bertie and Daisy. Suddenly they both stopped dead at a frozen puddle. Bertie was down on his knees getting a really close look, while Daisy jumped up in excitement.

Just as Penny went over to see what they were up to, Bertie gave the puddle a great lick. Then suddenly he started running around yelping as though his tongue was on

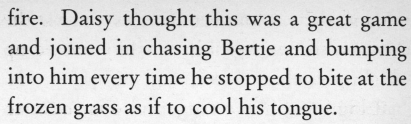

fire. Daisy thought this was a great game and joined in chasing Bertie and bumping into him every time he stopped to bite at the frozen grass as if to cool his tongue.

Penny started to panic. She thought Bertie might have licked something poisonous. She nearly slipped on the ice in her hurry to discover just what he had found.

Luckily there was no poison, but sitting miserably in the middle of the frozen puddle was a small toad. He was trying to move away but his feet were firmly stuck to the ice. Toads can give off a nasty taste to stop other animals eating them. Bertie's friendly lick had given him a mouthful of nasty taste. Still, it would not do him any harm. Penny almost laughed with relief. But now she was worried about the little toad.

He was about four centimetres long with a knobbly brownish skin so different from the bright, shiny green skin of a frog. He had big eyes, like a frog, and kept closing one and then the other in his efforts to pull first one foot, then another, away from the ice. Penny noticed that his nose did not look right. She could not be sure, but thought to herself, "I can't remember toads having big, red lumps on the ends of their noses."

She decided that the toad, who she immediately christened Rudolf, really did need looking at and should go to St. Tiggys to have that lump checked. But Penny could not get Rudolf off the ice, and as she touched him he huffed and puffed. Either his feet were sore, or he was having a temper tantrum! Penny knew she would have to take the whole sheet of ice off the puddle and wait for it to thaw out before she could get Rudolf properly checked over.

She picked up the ice and, with Bertie and Daisy keeping well behind, carried it to her car, with Rudolf sitting on it like a king on his throne. But before she got to St Tiggy's, the ice sheet melted away to a puddle in the passenger seat and Rudolf had disappeared. He must have hopped off while Penny was concentrating on driving. She was scared that he might crawl over to her side of the car and get squashed under one of the pedals, so she stopped the car in a field gateway, and searched for him. She found him, his little nose almost glowing, sitting right in front of Bertie and Daisy who were fast asleep on the back seat. As Penny had nothing really safe to keep him in, she picked him up and put him in the glove compartment so that he couldn't go for any more walks.

I was very surprised when Penny arrived with the little toad. I could only imagine that his winter bed must have been disturbed and that he had just been trying to take a swim when he got frozen on to the puddle. I was pleased that I could do something to help him. I like toads.

I took him from Penny and he tried to give the little squeaky croak that male toads give, but he only managed to silently puff himself up. He seemed to be all right and his feet were not sore from the ice, but he did have this funny lump on the end of his nose which was stopping his squeaky croaks getting out.

I had a few ideas what the lump might be so I took him through to the prep room, where we carry out all our first aid, to have a really good look at it. It could easily have been frostbite but as I touched it with a pair of tweezers Rudolf tried another squeaky croak, and I could tell that the lump was really very painful. I tried to see if it was an abscess, which I could treat very easily, but it was too solid. I would have to get our specialist vet, Dr John, to look at it . And of course he could operate on Rudolf if he thought the lump would cause him any problems.

For now, I tucked Rudolf into one of our frog and toad intensive-care aquariums. I thought he might like a swim, but as soon as I put him into the shallow water at one end he promptly clambered out on to the gravel bank at the opposite end. I had the very things that would cheer him up and settle him down – fat, juicy waxworms. Waxworms are like giant white maggots. We may think they're pretty awful but animals like toads, bats and even swallows look on them as "Big Mags", their favourite treat.

I put the first one down in front of Rudolf and watched his reaction to its slow wriggling. He saw it straight away and stood up as tall as he could and stared at it without moving. Then ever so slowly he picked up one front foot and moved a little nearer, still staring unblinking at the waxworm. And then "whoosh!" – it disappeared so fast I didn't even see it. I only knew that he had caught it because toads cannot swallow like us; they have to move their food down their throats by closing their eyes and pushing down from the inside. Rudolf closed his eyes and stretched his neck forward as the waxworm went down. Then he opened his eyes and his empty mouth as if to lick his lips and say, "Scrummy! Can I have another one?" Altogether he ate six waxworms, one after the other. I thought he was going to burst. Then he had had enough, and crawled backwards underneath a rock to sleep off his big dinner. He must have felt a lot better, even with his sore nose.

When Dr John came he fell in love with Rudolf just like the rest of us. He thought Rudolf's lump was some sort of infection and said he would have to cut a little bit of it away, so that he could get it tested in a laboratory. (This test is called a biopsy.) Cutting a piece of the lump away was obviously going to be painful so John anaesthetised Rudolf so that he would be in a deep sleep and would not feel a thing.

Because toads are cold-blooded, unlike humans, it took Rudolf a long time to wake up after the anaesthetic. We were all worried but before long he had come round. He was obviously perfectly all right

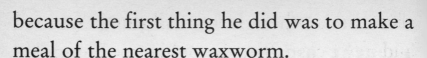

because the first thing he did was to make a meal of the nearest waxworm.

Having got the results of the biopsy, John put in a system of treatments. Rudolf had a "fungal granuloma" (a lump to you and me). By the twelfth day of Christmas, Rudolf's nose was back to normal and completely healed. We could not release him back to the wild until winter was over, but by March the weather would be mild enough.

It's on warm, rainy nights in March that toads leave their winter homes and head for a familiar pond in which to breed. Somehow they always find their way back to the very pond where they grew up as tadpoles. Obviously we could not put Rudolf back in the little puddle where Bertie and Daisy found him, but another of our volunteers, Julie, has a garden full of nice ponds where we put all our frog, toad and newt casualties once they are better.

On the first rainy evening in March, we took Rudolf to Julie's garden. There were already lots of toads there, all looking for a suitable mate. Rudolf seemed to have the right idea. As soon as I put him on to a lily pad he dived in and swam over to the first toad he saw. Unfortunately, the toad he'd picked on was another male who gave out the squeaky croak as soon as Rudolf touched him. Rudolf could not let go fast enough and swam off, embarrassed, to look elsewhere.

And then he saw her - a big toad nearly four times his size and a lot more knobbly. It was love at first sight. To Julie and I she looked fat, brown and lumpy but to Rudolf she was beautiful. And she did not squeak or croak when he grabbed hold of her. I

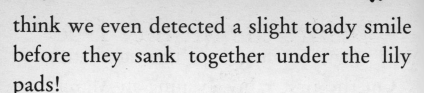

think we even detected a slight toady smile before they sank together under the lily pads!

After all his troubles through the winter, Rudolf had found peace at last. He would now treat Julie's pond as his home and would return every spring to find Mrs Rudolf and have thousands more baby tadpoles. And every Christmas, we would remember Rudolf the red-nosed toad.

Deidre the Mother Deer

Muntjac are tiny deer about the size of a small sheep. Most of them live around Buckinghamshire where people love to see them in the woods and even in their gardens. Unfortunately, muntjac are really silly deer and have no road sense whatsoever. Every day accident casualties are brought to St. Tiggywinkles for help.

In spite of their small size, muntjac are very strong and fight like tigers. Deidre was no exception. She arrived at the Hospital sitting quietly on the passenger seat of a car. John Sissons, the driver, had found her lying by the side of the busy Aylesbury to Amersham road. She seemed to have been hit by a car.

She looked all sweet and gentle, as if butter would not melt in her mouth, but when I first touched her to pick her up, she went mad. She screamed as though she was being murdered and kicked me with all her might. She ripped right through my sweatshirt and T-shirt with her sharp hooves, and even grazed my skin. Then her hard little head came up and hit me WHAM! under my chin. I bit my tongue which really hurt. I don't know how I managed to hang on to her because all the time she was wriggling like a giant eel.

Eventually I staggered with her into the treatment room. I sat down and held her across my lap, while Lisa gave the crazy deer some sedative to calm her.

I think I needed a sedative too! I was in a terrible state: sweating, gasping for breath, covered in hair with my sweatshirt and T-shirt torn to shreds and two angry-looking grazes down my side where her sharp hooves had caught me.

After about ten minutes, Deidre settled right down so I laid her on a blanket

It wasn't until Lisa called out, "Who's bleeding, you or the deer?" that I realised I was in a worse state than I'd thought. I looked down and, for the first time, saw the gaping hole where the deer had somehow managed to kick me between the fingers. Blood dripped on to the floor and I could feel myself getting hotter and the room start to spin around. I sat down on the floor next to Deidre and put my head between my

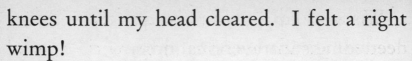

knees until my head cleared. I felt a right wimp!

When I felt better, I washed my hand under the tap. Now I knew the wound was there, it began to hurt. I could see that it was going to need stitching.

Lisa offered to stitch it for me. "After all," she said, "we're always stitching up hedgehogs."

"They're braver than me," I said, wrapping a temporary bandage around my hand to stop the bleeding. "I'm not letting any of you lot near my valuable skin. As soon as Deidre's sorted out, I'm off to the human hospital!"

Deidre was now sitting calmly on the floor and looking up at me as if to say, "What's all the fuss about? I've been hit by a car and I'm not making any noise. Not now, anyway."

We worked quickly and quietly. Deidre needed an intravenous drip with special medicines to help her over the shock of her accident. Her front leg was broken, so I quickly plastered it to keep it still.

While we were doing this I noticed that she was having trouble breathing, so I took some X-rays of her chest which Lisa developed while I comforted Deidre.

Thankfully they showed that she had not injured her chest or lungs, but they showed us something else: the outline of a tiny head. Deidre was pregnant!

Now we had to make sure that the tiny baby she was carrying was all right. I had bought a very special stethoscope from America with which I could listen to the faintest sounds and heartbeats inside animals. While Deidre was still quiet, I knelt down and listened to her heartbeat.

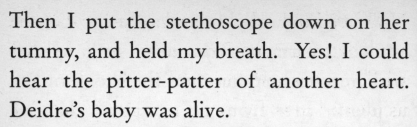

Then I put the stethoscope down on her tummy, and held my breath. Yes! I could hear the pitter-patter of another heart. Deidre's baby was alive.

I called to the nurses, "Everything's OK! We're going to be a mother!"

There was terrific excitement, and one by one, everybody listened to the tiny heart beating. Deidre did not seem to mind.

Carefully now, I carried Deidre out of the hospital building down to the deer intensive-care area. She did not fight or kick this time and soon settled down amongst the cosy, warm hay. The next twenty-four hours were going to be crucial.

After sorting Deidre out, I went to get my hand sorted out at the local hospital for humans. I was going to pull through!

All that night and all the following day we took it in turns to check on Deidre.

Now we knew she was a mother-to-be, she got star treatment. The nurses even fed her with peaches and apricots. Each time one of us peeked in she was sitting calmly chewing the cud. Deer, including muntjac, are ruminants, and like cows, digest their food twice. They eat a lot and then when they are sitting quietly, they bring up balls of undigested food into their mouths and grind it down with their specially flattened back teeth. They swallow it again and it goes down into another one of their four stomachs. This chewing of the cud meant that Deidre was happy and settled.

We had no way of knowing when Deidre's baby was due to be born, and we were worried in case the accident might cause it to be born too early. One of the problems was that every third day I had to catch Deidre and take her in to have her

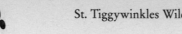

plaster changed, so it didn't rub her or cause any swelling. I tried to be very gentle and not hurt her or the baby growing inside her. But Deidre took great delight in kicking me, tearing my clothes and head-butting me until my chin was black and blue. And she still screamed even though I knew I was not hurting her. I was becoming a nervous wreck and dreaded the days when Lisa would call me and say, "Time to change Deidre's plaster."

Through all this pandemonium, Deidre was getting fitter and stronger, and every time I brought her in we could hear the pitter-patter of her baby's heart. Then one Wednesday morning, when I went down to grapple with her once again, there, sitting in the far corner of her shed, was the prettiest little deer you could ever wish to see. It was no bigger than a puppy, with big, black eyes and chubby, furry little cheeks topped with a little button nose that wrinkled trying to pick up my scent as I looked in. The baby deer was light brown and covered in white spots just like a proper Bambi. Deidre seemed to be totally ignoring her baby, but she had spotted me, and ran at the door which I only just closed in time.

Everybody was excited over the baby and all took turns to peek at it through a crack in the shed door. We could not tell if it was a boy or a girl, but for now assumed it was a little buck, and called it "Dapple".

You would have thought that now the baby was born, our worries would all be over. But there were still a few hurdles to cross; mainly, would Deidre feed her baby properly and how on earth was I going to get her out to have her plaster changed now!

Over the next few days, we all took turns

at peeking in to see if Dapple was feeding. But each time he was sitting in the corner while Deidre stood guard at the door. I did not try to change her plaster for a few days just so she and her baby could get to know one another and form the bond that is so important between animals and their young. The good news was that the baby seemed completely fit and well, so we could assume that he was being fed when we were not looking.

Then the day came when I really did have to change Deidre's plaster. What worried me was that she might hurt Dapple during our wrestling match. The first thing muntjac do in panic is jump straight up in the air. Sure enough, Deidre did just this. Fortunately, I managed to catch her before she came down again on top of Dapple – she was at least a little bit lighter now that she had had her baby! She still kicked though, but instead of that unearthly screaming she just let out little soft squeaks. Dapple answered her, but did not move from his corner.

Thankfully, Deidre's leg was much better. I would now only need to change the plaster every two weeks. I was getting tired of our wrestling matches, and looking forward to the final one. I am sure that Deidre felt exactly the same way.

After another four weeks, I took Deidre's plaster off for the last time. Her leg had healed beautifully but it was now a lot thicker, with extra bone that had grown to protect the injury site. At first she could not get used to not having the weight of the plaster and would lift her leg right up off the ground as she walked. She took a day or two to get used to it and then had a slight limp that, I knew, she would have for some time.

I decided it was time for mother and baby to go outside into our small deer enclosure. Deidre was obviously being a very good mother. Dapple was now almost as big as Deidre and, judging from his rushes at the door, was just as scatty. I went in to catch Deidre. As usual she leapt up into the air and, as I caught her, kicked out at me. I carried her to the paddock as quickly as possible and happily let her go. Now for the baby!

I had never handled Dapple before but I caught him too, as he jumped straight up in the air like a pogo stick. He nearly escaped my clutches as I carried him kicking and struggling to join his mother. He was surprisingly strong for such a little deer.

Quickly I got into the paddock while Lisa

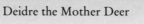
closed the gate behind me. I put Dapple down on the first green grass he had ever seen. He looked a bit shaky and unsure of himself but a soft squeak from Deidre set him running off towards his mum, giving out little squeaks of delight. They nuzzled each other and trotted off amongst the plants.

As I went out and closed the gate, Lisa pointed to my sweatshirt and laughed, "Even the baby has managed to tear your clothes." I had not realised before, that muntjac babies are taught by their mothers to tear clothes. Judging by the number of muntjac coming into the hospital every week, I was going to have to buy a whole new wardrobe.

Deidre and Dapple will stay in the paddock for about another eight weeks until Deidre's leg is much stronger, and her young buck can look after himself.

Why did the Chicken Cross the Road?

At St. Tiggywinkles we never know who is going to turn up in the next cardboard box brought into casualty reception. Bernard arrived with Lucy, who had rescued him while out shopping with her mother. He was a fluffy yellow chick found "cheeping" in the gutter in Aylesbury High Street. Lia, who runs the bird nursery, immediately fell for this cuddly bundle. Bernard went "Cheep, cheep" at her because he thought she was his mother.

Lia already had a little fluffy duckling called Matt in her nursery. She thought it would be a good idea if they grew up together. She put them in a big warm cage together, and as neither of them had a mother, Lia gave them a feather duster in place of one. They loved their new feathery mother and went straight under her and snuggled down together in the warmth.

Bernard was the first to come out and, in true chicken fashion, he started to peck anything on the floor of his cage that might possibly be food. All the time he was calling "Cheep, cheep, cheep", until finally Matt could not resist a wander round to see what he could find to eat. He found the water fountain, and for the first time discovered he was a duck. He dabbled, paddled and splashed Bernard with water.

Bernard didn't take too kindly to this – perhaps he had just discovered that he was a chicken.

Under Lia's care, Matt and Bernard grew and grew until they were soon bigger than their feather duster. They looked very silly trying to get under it to sleep at night! They thought that if their heads were covered, they could not be seen, but their little bottoms would stick out all night long.

Matt loved being a duck and practically lived in the water fountain. He got himself and everything else around him soaking wet. Lia kept a very close watch on his antics because baby ducks are not waterproof and can catch a chill. At least three times a day, Matt had to be dried off with a hair drier. Once even Bernard had to be blow-dried when he tried his luck at swimming!

The two of them became very attached to each other. They grew bigger and stronger, and their fluffy yellow feathers turned dark. Now Bernard really did look like a chicken, and Matt looked like a proper duck. Matt was growing proper duck wings which helped him splash water even further around his cage. But as they grew I could see that he had a problem. The ends of his wings were growing out sideways, and sticking out like aeroplane wings. This condition is actually known as "aeroplane wing" and it affects a lot of ducks, geese and swans. If they are born like this they have it for the rest of their lives and will never fly. There is nothing that can be done about it. It looked as though Matt would always live with Bernard. He could never fly away to find other ducks to splash around with.

Down the corridor from the nursery at

St. Tiggywinkles is the bird intensive-care unit. In here I had another duck. His name was Ed. He was a big, portly white Aylesbury duck who had broken his leg probably because he was too fat. He was a real moaner. He moaned a scolding of soft quacks, "waack waack", when you looked at him. He moaned "waack waack" even when you talked to him. He moaned "waack waack" when you put his food or water in. I don't know what he had to moan about – he ate and drank more than any other bird in the hospital.

True, he did have a broken leg, but we were trying to mend that. There was no reason to bite Jane when she attempted to give him his medicine pills.

Ed would never fly either. Aylesbury ducks cannot fly. Anyway, he was probably too fat to take off! He was walking about on his broken leg which was healing nicely. When finally I took the plaster cast off, the leg was as strong as ever, though a little thicker than before.

At first Ed could not get used to his leg being so light. He kept toppling over on to his back, waving his feet in the air. We had to keep putting him back up the right way and each time he moaned more than ever. Finally, after a whole day of trying, he managed to stay upright. Now all he had was a slight limp which looked really funny as he walked his big, fat roly-poly walk towards any food that was on offer.

All this time Ed had been on his own. I decided that now was the time to introduce him to Bernard and Matt. We have a large safe garden area at the back of the hospital, with high walls all around it.

One bright sunny morning, we put the

three of them in the walled garden together. In true chicken manner, Bernard immediately started scratching the ground and pecking up any morsels he could find. Matt ran over, jumped straight into the large water bowl and started splashing about. This time it did not matter how much mess he made. Meanwhile, Ed waddled after them going "Waack waack!" as if to say, "Oi! Slow down, you two!"

They took a little while to get used to each other, but the "pecking order" was soon established. Bernard was the leader. As he darted about exploring the garden, Matt and Ed followed in single file, Matt with his poor wings sticking out sideways and big fat Ed waddling after, trying to keep up and moaning non-stop.

The three of them soon settled into their new home, and became great friends. They went everywhere together, and at night they slept huddled up in a heap, their heads resting on one another. Usually we find homes for non-wild animals, but there was no way we could split these three up. Besides, everybody at St. Tiggys loved them. I decided to let them stay with us in the walled garden.

As the days passed, we noticed that sometimes Bernard was not with the other two. But after searching all over, Sue spotted him sitting in a dark corner in their little hut. We thought nothing more of it until one day, as I was cleaning the hut out, I spotted a neat pile of soft chicken feathers in the corner. Right in the middle were four bright shiny new chicken eggs. So Bernard was not a cock bird at all, he was a hen. Just shows how much I know about chickens! I should have called her Bernice – but it was too late now, we couldn't think of calling her anything other than Bernard after all this time!

Bernard was very proud of her eggs and crowed loudly every time she laid one. It was sad that they were never going to hatch as Bernard needed a cockerel to make them fertile. But she was not unhappy, for although she did not have a cockerel, she had Ed. After only a few days in the walled garden, Ed had fallen madly in love with her. At every opportunity he would climb on her as if he were a cockerel. It was a wonder she was not flattened – though she was getting a bare patch where Ed would use his beak trying to hold on. Matt was not the slightest bit interested in their relationship. Instead, he took to sitting on Bernard's eggs for her and would take great delight in getting off the nest so that she could lay another one.

The three of them seemed to have sorted out their bizarre relationship and liked their home in the walled garden. Then we introduced another visitor to the happy threesome: a pretty white duck who had been attacked by a dog. When we had stitched up all her wounds and she was healed and strong, we put her in the walled garden. We watched, with fingers crossed, as Ed made his usual "Waack, waack" hello, but really they were not at all interested. In fact, they were very rude, and waddled off together to check Bernard's eggs, leaving "D", the new duck, looking sad and dejected.

Day after day she tried to join the other three but they just turned their backs on her. D took to looking after the wild duckling orphans we were always rearing in the walled garden. They obviously thought that she was much better than a feather duster and we found that they grew much quicker thanks to her dedication.

Little did we know that D had a trick up her sleeve, or should I say, under her wing. While nobody was paying any attention, she had quietly built herself a nest in amongst some thistles and had started laying eggs. She did not crow about it like Bernard. None of the others realised the eggs were there until Bernard tripped over them one day, and called the other two over. D was very proud of her eggs and stood there tidying up little bits of the feather nest as if she were dusting a nursery. All this was too much for Ed, who straight away fell in love with D, too. Ed was the biggest of the three and you could almost hear him threatening the other two in his own grumpy waack-waack voice, "I think we ought to let D into our gang. After all, four is an even number." Bernard and Matt were too interested in their own egg-laying to bother answering.

Now all four of them waddle around the garden in line. Bernard is in front followed by Matt with his poor wings. Next comes roly-poly Ed, followed by an adoring elegant white duck called D.

By the way –
Why did the chicken cross the road?
To get to St. Tiggywinkles, of course.

Tips from St. Tiggywinkles

1. Don't leave litter, especially empty bottles, cans or string lying around, where wild animals can get trapped.

2. If you have tadpoles in your garden pond, make sure that when they change into froglets, they can climb out of the water.

3. Don't catch butterflies or moths as their wings are easily damaged.

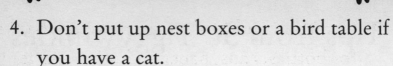

4. Don't put up nest boxes or a bird table if you have a cat.

5. If you find an injured wild animal or bird, get a grown-up to telephone your local rescue centre, or St. Tiggywinkles for help.

6. Put small injured wild animals or birds in a cardboard box and cover it with a towel. DO NOT give them anything to drink. Then get them taken to your local rescue centre STRAIGHT AWAY.

7. Get everybody you know to plant at least one British species of tree or bush.

8. Check out your parents' garage where open tins of paint or oil may be a trap for hedgehogs, birds and insects.

9. Get Mum and Dad to use recycling banks
    for bottles, cans, paper and other waste.
    This will save animals from injury and
    preserve some of the Earth's resources.

10. Join Tiggy's Club and learn about
    projects that could help the birds and
    animals in your garden.

The address is:
        St. Tiggywinkles,
        Aylesbury,
        Bucks
        HP17 8AF

There's a video about St. Tiggywinkles, too!

From Tempo Video.
Available in all good video shops